Miguel's FAMILY

BY ELLIOT RILEY

ILLUSTRATED BY
SRIMALIE BASSANI

Rourke
Educational Media
rourkeeducationalmedia.com

Scan for Related Titles
and Teacher Resources

Before & After Reading Activities

Teaching Focus:

Concepts of Print: Have students find capital letters and punctuation in a sentence. Ask students to explain the purpose for using them in a sentence.

Before Reading:

Building Academic Vocabulary and Background Knowledge

Before reading a book, it is important to set the stage for your child or student by using pre-reading strategies. This will help them develop their vocabulary, increase their reading comprehension, and make connections across the curriculum.

1. Read the title and look at the cover. *Let's make predictions about what this book will be about.*
2. Take a picture walk by talking about the pictures/photographs in the book. Implant the vocabulary as you take the picture walk. Be sure to talk about the text features such as headings, the Table of Contents, glossary, bolded words, captions, charts/ diagrams, or Index.
3. Have students read the first page of text with you then have students read the remaining text.
4. Strategy Talk – use to assist students while reading.
   - Get your mouth ready
   - Look at the picture
   - Think…does it make sense
   - Think…does it look right
   - Think…does it sound right
   - Chunk it – by looking for a part you know
5. Read it again.

Content Area Vocabulary
Use glossary words in a sentence.

audience
character
gathers
stage

After Reading:

Comprehension and Extension Activity

After reading the book, work on the following questions with your child or students in order to check their level of reading comprehension and content mastery.

1. *What do Miguel and his sisters do for fun? (Summarize)*
2. *Do Miguel's family members live close to each other?(Asking Questions)*
3. *How is Miguel's family like yours? How is it different? (Text to self connection)*
4. *Do all families enjoy doing the same things? (Asking Questions)*

Extension Activity

Have an adult help you find two or three old magazines or catalogs. Look for pictures of families and cut them out. Glue the family pictures on a piece of paper to make a family collage.

Table of Contents

Meet Miguel

This is Miguel.

Miguel lives with his parents, sisters, and grandparents.

His aunts, uncles, and cousins live nearby.

Everyone **gathers** to play and cook together.

Story Time

Miguel and his sisters like to make up stories.

They create costumes for each story **character**.

Show Time

They act out the stories on a **stage**.

Miguel's family gathers to watch the show.

14

Their friends and neighbors come, too.

16

Miguel sees many families in the **audience**. They laugh and clap.

Miguel and his sisters take a bow. *Bravo! Bravo!*

Miguel loves his family.

Miguel's family loves Miguel.

Picture Glossary

 **audience** (AW-dee-uhns): People who watch a performance.

 **character** (KAR-ik-tur): The people in a story, book, or show.

 **gathers** (gaTH-urs): Comes together in a group.

 **stage** (stayj): A raised platform that actors perform on.

Family Fun

Who are the people in your family?

Draw each person and write their name below their picture.

How is your family portrait like Miguel's? How is it different?

About the Author

Elliot Riley is an author with a big family of her own in Tampa, Florida. She loves when everyone gets together to eat, laugh, and play games. Especially the eating part!

Meet The Author!
www.meetREMauthors.com

Library of Congress PCN Data

Miguel's Family/ Elliot Riley
(All Kinds of Families)
ISBN 978-1-68342-147-4 (hard cover)
ISBN 978-1-68342-189-4 (soft cover)
ISBN 978-1-68342-219-8 (e-Book)
Library of Congress Control Number: 2016956512

Rourke Educational Media
Printed in the United States of America,
North Mankato, Minnesota

www.rourkeeducationalmedia.com
Author Illustration: ©Robert Wicher
Edited by: Keli Sipperley
Cover design and interior design by:
Rhea Magaro-Wallace

Also Available as:

ROURKE'S e-Books